There Was A Crooked Man

Ple.

Y

Yo

Retold by Russell Punter

Illustrated by David Semple

There was a crooked man

and he walked
a crooked mile.

He found a crooked sixpence,
upon a crooked stile.

He bought
a crooked cat

which caught a crooked mouse.

And they all lived together

in a little crooked house.

The crooked man
was hungry.

So he cooked
a crooked fish.

His crooked
cat could
smell it.

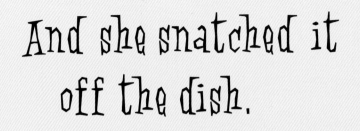

And she snatched it
off the dish.

The crooked man was **angry**.

He chased his cat outside.

He couldn't see her anywhere.

She'd found
a place to hide.

The man smelled something fishy,

so he followed
where it led...

into his crooked shed.

snuggled up against each other

were thirteen hungry kittens

and their kind
but crooked mother.

Edited by Jenny Tyler and Lesley Sims

First published in 2013 by Usborne Publishing Ltd., Usborne House, 83-85 Saffron Hill,
London EC1N 8RT, England. www.usborne.com Copyright © 2013 Usborne Publishing Ltd.